I'M SO GRUMPY!

Copyright © 2008 by Hans Wilhelm, Inc.

All rights reserved. Published by Scholastic Inc.
SCHOLASTIC, CARTWHEEL BOOKS, NOODLES, and associated logos
are trademarks and/or registered trademarks of Scholastic Inc.
Lexile is a registered trademark of MetaMetrics, Inc.

Library of Congress Cataloging-in-Publication Data is available.

ISBN 978-0-545-07076-8

12 11 10 9 8 7 6   11 12 13 14 15/0

Printed in the U.S.A. 40 • This edition first printing, June 2010

I'M SO GRUMPY!

by Hans Wilhelm

Cartwheel
·B·O·O·K·S·®

SCHOLASTIC INC.

New York   Toronto   London   Auckland
Sydney   Mexico City   New Delhi   Hong Kong

I feel grumpy.
Stay out of my way!

This food is boring.

I don't want
to go outside!

Let go of me!
I don't want to be brushed.

Why won't everyone leave me alone?

Get off my pillow!

Today is not a good day.

Get away from me!

Waaaaah!

Now we're both grumpy.

I'm tired of being grumpy.
It's no fun.

I know what I need!

Come here, Baby.

Tickle me.

Ha, ha!
Hee, hee!
A good tickle always
makes me laugh.

Now we're not
grumpy anymore.